Goldie Is Mad

Written and Illustrated by

Margie Palatini

SCHOLASTIC INC.

New York Toronto London Auckland Sydney
Mexico City New Delhi Hong Kong Buenos Aires

ISBN 0-439-36642-9

12 11 10   5 6 7/0

Printed in the U.S.A.   23

First Scholastic printing, December 2002

This book is set in 36-point Guardi.

I'm Goldie.

I'm **mad**.

Mad, mad, mad!

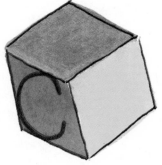

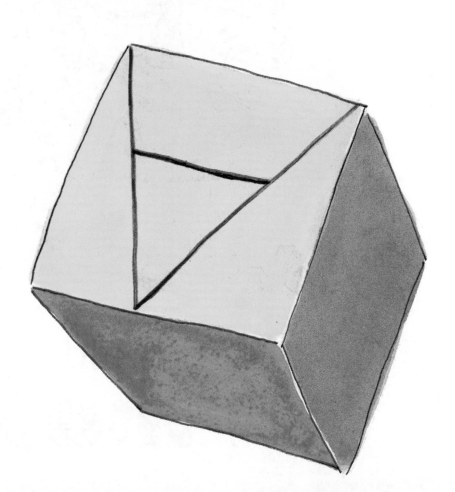

Nicholas took Veronica.

He sucked her hair.

Veronica hates
baby spit.

I hate baby spit.

I **hate**
Nicholas!

Uh-oh.
Veronica got
a time-out.

Uh-oh.
Me, too.

We have to think
and be sorry.

But, we don't think
we are sorry.

We think we still
hate Nicholas!

Veronica thinks that Nicholas should disappear.

Me, too.

Ta-da!

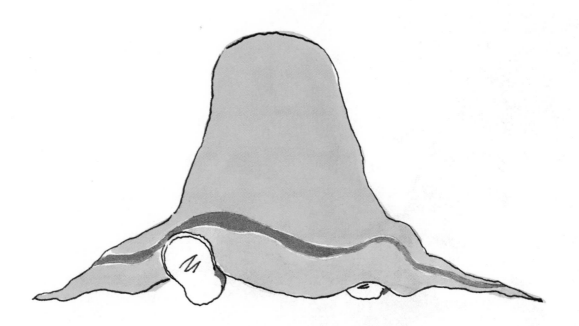

No more Nicholas!

Uh-oh.
No more Nicholas?

But sometimes
Nicholas is silly.
Veronica likes that.

Me, too.

Nicholas smells nice after a bath.
Veronica likes that.

Me, too.

And he gives good hugs . . .
for a little brother.

Veronica likes that, too.

Veronica thinks she needs
to think some more.

Me, too.

Veronica thinks she doesn't really hate baby spit.

OR Nicholas.

I think
Veronica
is sorry.

Me, too.

I think.